tuxedo's
~~tails~~ tales

Written by Tuxedo Hess

Illustrated by Katie Tunn

D0495560

About this book

I take it you must be a lover of horses, which is a good start for both of us. I'm one of those... a horse, that is, and my name is Tuxedo.

I'm a Criollo from Argentina. As you can see from the cover of my book, I'm black with a white stripe down the middle of my nose, which gives me a rather distinguished look, don't you think?

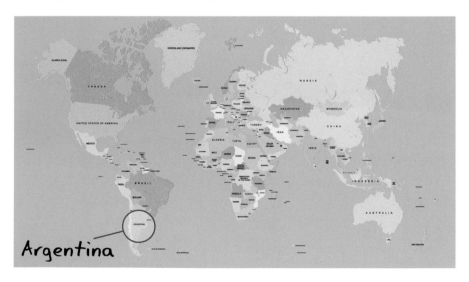

Argentina

So, I hear you asking, where is Argentina?

Well, it is in South America. My breed has been described as "the hardiest horses around" and we are descendants from the conquistadors. Anyway, enough of the history lesson.

tuxedo's ~~taits~~ tales

"Why am I writing my book?" you ask.

Well, I've had quite a turbulent life, some good times and some not so very good, but I am very lucky. My new mum rescued and looked after me in Malaysia. She and I then moved to the UK, which has made me the horse that I am today. Therefore, with this in mind, I wish to share my private stories and experiences with you that I've had over the past twelve months enjoying the countryside and wildlife that lives within it.

At the end of each chapter are my little pearls of wisdom – these are for you to think about and use on a daily basis or when you think is appropriate.

I hope you enjoy reading my tales and being able to share them with your family and friends.

Love n hoof hugs,

Contents of stories

Russell the Robin
and understanding the meaning of sharing

White fluffy stuff, being shod
meeting Jeremy, Charlotte and Jessica

My scars
Howard the Hare and primroses

Lambs, candle trees
April showers and rainbows

Meeting Picasso
exercise, wild garlic, bluebells and badgers

Meadow flowers
meeting Simon the Bee and the noise
coming from the Quiet Garden

Butterflies, moles
meeting Jeremy again

Streams, monsters
being washed and the night sky

Exercise
nutrition and conkers

changing of the leaves
the mud incident and meeting Romeo

Losing friends, having fun
dealing with anger and coping with sadness

the stable christmas party
and meeting the man in the red suit

Here
are some
of my
friends.

Can you
remember
all their
names?

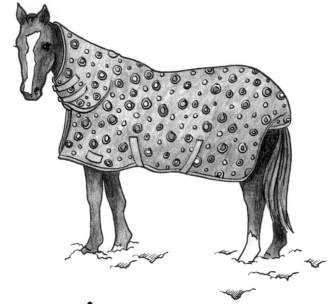

Russell the Robin

and understanding the meaning of sharing

W ell, I hope you all got some amazing Christmas presents from Father Christmas.

I got a new thick winter rug (which is like a very snugly duvet) along with a halter and lead rope in rather fetching colours. I have to tell you about the colours in my rug first – it has a dark brown background with really bright blue and pink spots on it. I look like a haribo all-sort. The halter and lead rope are both in matching electric blue. How trendy am I?

I need my winter rug as it gets very cold at night. I know this as I can see my breath as I breathe out through my nose.

While I was standing in my stable, waiting for the sun to rise, out from the dark, I heard: "Hello, you're very tall, and you have very big feet, and you have four of them. I've only got two legs and they are very thin." All this was said very quickly in a high-pitched voice.

I couldn't see anything; then I felt a slight breeze across my face, which startled me, so I stood back and snorted as I didn't know what it was. Then the same high-pitched voice said, "Sorry to have frightened you, but I'm over here on the top of your stable door."

So I walked over, adjusting my eyes to the light, and there I saw a small round ball with thin legs and a sharp-looking nose.

"Good morning," I said. "I'm Tuxedo, and who are you?" The sun by this time was starting to come up, and I could see how beautiful this funny, feathered, talking ball looked. The most striking thing about it was its bright red breast.

The round ball introduced himself. "I'm Russell the Robin, meaning 'little red one' – bet you didn't know that, oh tall one – and I'm the bird of winter."

"No, I didn't know that, Russell. Very pleased to meet you and the reason why I'm a little taller than you is because I'm a horse," I said.

With that, Russell did that breeze thing again, bringing his wings together and flapping them at the same time very fast, which made him move in front of my nose, making me sneeze again. He explained that's how birds get around and it's called flying.

"It's an amazing feeling," said Russell. "You should try it," he said, looking at me; then he looked at my big hoofs and said, "Perhaps not." He then took it upon himself to fly and landed inside my food bucket, and started eating my leftover dinner, which I had been saving for later. I must admit I thought it was a bit rude of him, especially without asking.

In between mouthfuls, Russell explained that it was called a beak, not a nose, and that in the winter months food was hard to find. Due to the harsh frosts and the cold winter weather, he needed to keep his strength up to build the nest (that's a bird home) ready for the new family of chicks to hatch and grow before they are ready to fly away to have their own adventures.

Therefore, he really appreciated any food he could get. While he was explaining this to me, I totally understood where he was coming from, as before my new mum looked after me I hadn't been fed enough and sometimes had been hungry too. I'd forgotten what it felt like to have a rumbly tum.

While I was thinking, on how much my life had improved for the better, I saw two bright lights beaming down the road coming towards my stable, announcing the arrival of Mum.

I always love this time of day with her. She gives me a big cuddle along with my favourite breakfast of carrots, so to thank her I give her lots of carrot kisses (carrot kisses are when I lick Mum's face after I've finished eating them) to show my love. In the winter, I'm in my stable in the evenings so I'm not in the cold wind and rain. During the day, I'm in my field where I spend the day munching on grass and playing with my friends.

In the mornings, I'm always the first one out into my field, which I love. First thing I do is to snort, kick up my back legs and run around to get warm. That sense of running is such fun and sometimes the early mornings can be quite cold. This morning was no exception. After running around for a couple of minutes I had warmed up nicely.

So with that done, it was grass-eating time – for us horses a very important part of the day. As I'm enjoying the dawn, the sun is waking up to start her new day; with that the rabbits hopped over to say good morning.

The rabbits are Tom, Gina and Patsy. Tom, being the older brother, has a black nose, a deep voice and one ear longer than the other. Gina, the middle sister, has a slight stutter, but that doesn't stop her from being a tomboy along with being very inquisitive and asking lots of questions and generally being bossy. Then there's sweet Patsy, the younger sister, who has big, loving, brown eyes, tiny paws and is quite shy. She has a very gentle and loving nature about her, always caring for others, quite different to her boisterous and protective brother and sister.

"Morning, Tuxedo, what are you up to today, trying to keep warm and dry? I think it's going to rain quite heavily later today," said Tom, being the authoritative one on all things weather-wise.

"That's the plan," I said. "You'll never guess who I met today."

"Who?" said Gina, who liked to know all the gossip of the day. As I was about to explain my morning meeting with Russell, a thundering of hoofs started coming towards us, announcing the arrival of Mercy, who is my next-door neighbour throughout the year, along with being one of my best horse friends.

With a whinny, Mercy greeted everyone with a loud "Good morning, all".

Mercy is a retired racehorse now enjoying the quiet life. Mind you, you wouldn't think that the way he gallops around his field. He's a little taller than me and has a chestnut-coloured (light orangey-brown) coat, mane and tail.

"So what have I missed?" asked Mercy.

"Tuxedo was about to tell us who he met this morning," said Tom.

"I met Russell earlier this morning, he's a robin. I couldn't see him at first, as it was too dark. He came into my stable to introduce himself, nice chap," I said. "He's got an amazing red-coloured breast, looked quite regal."

"He's the cute bird of winter, isn't he? What was he doing there?" asked Gina.

"He was hungry," I replied. "He couldn't find any food, but he needs to eat so he has the energy to build a nest for his children who will be here soon."

"And did you give him some food?" asked Patsy.

"Of course he did," said Mercy. "Tuxedo is the most generous horse I know – he'll share everything and anything with anyone."

"That's nice of you to say, Mercy. Yes, I did share my dinner with him as Mum always gives me a lot and I remember what it felt like to be hungry – you know that feeling of a rumbly empty tum. So I've invited Russell to have dinner with me every night so he's sure of getting the food he needs, keeping him strong so he is able to build his nest."

With that the sun was getting higher in the sky, but in the distance some dark clouds were forming, so Tom was right about the approaching rain.

Little Pearl of Wisdom for January

To share your friendship with others, if you see someone or an animal who is less fortunate than you, offer them part of your sandwich, a couple of your sweets or something that you know they would enjoy. Nobody likes to be hungry.

Make sure you share your cuddles and affections with family and friends. Everyone loves a hug.

White fluffy stuff, being shod

meeting Jeremy, Charlotte and Jessica

When I woke up this morning the first thing I noticed was that it was very, very quiet, just completely silent. I popped my head out of my stable and I had to blink a few times.

I couldn't believe what I was seeing; I'd never seen anything like it. Everywhere I looked was covered in a thick white blanket making everything look very different.

With that, Russell the Robin popped in for his morning chat, explaining it was called snow. It was quite normal for this time of the year and it's really rather fun to play in. Then he did that Russell laugh as he does, a cheery sound, quite high-pitched, finishing off by saying, "But it is very, very cold."

So as you can imagine, while I was waiting for Mum, I had a mixture of two feelings: one of excitement and the other of nervousness, as I wasn't sure what to expect. I didn't have long to wait, as the two bright lights shining along the tree-lined avenue appeared, announcing

Mum's arrival. So after our morning kisses and cuddles we made our way up to my field. I can tell you I am so glad I have my bright thick rug on that I got for Christmas – it was so cold walking out this morning.

Walking in the snow at first felt like walking in sand, which I'd been used to when living overseas. The snow was quite deep and it made a slight squeaking sound as my hoofs went into it. I was beginning to get a little excited as the bottom of my legs were getting a slight tingly sensation, which felt very different to sand. Once we were in the field Mum took my head collar off and then my rug, which I thought was a little odd as it wasn't the warmest of mornings.

So here I was in the middle of my field, which looked totally transformed. At first, I was a little curious, sniffing at this very strange white stuff that had covered my field. It didn't smell of anything and it felt so light against my nose – in fact, it felt like cold sand. However, as some of the snow attached itself to my nose it gave me that tingly sensation that I'd felt at the bottom of my legs. I wanted to know what this feeling would feel like all over, so I pawed the snow with one of my front hoofs to make a hole and lowered all of my four legs to the ground, curling them tightly underneath me, allowing me to roll.

I rolled and rolled; left, right, right, left and repeated it so many times, it was an amazing feeling. I was having so much fun. But then it hit me – the cold, wow, it reenergised me so much that all I did was canter around my field. I bucked and reared and even snorted being just so, so happy I rolled and rolled and rolled again. I went quite berserk. Not realising how much energy I had, I felt so alive.

After a while I was becoming a little tired, so I had a rest from running around like a mad thing… and then it hit me – I got so cold

I had to stomp all of my hoofs very quickly to warm myself back up again. Mum had been watching me, knowing that I would get cold quite quickly once I'd stopped. So, she towelled me down, warming me up as she rubbed me and then put my new spotty rug back on. Ahh, that felt so much better. I began to warm back up immediately.

While I'd been stomping my hoofs, I'd woken up the rabbits, so they all hopped over to say hello, but as they did they sank into the snow, so all you could see were their little faces and ears popping up out of it. It looked very funny.

As we were all catching up with the morning news, I noticed some different markings in the snow. They didn't belong to the rabbits and they certainly weren't mine. They were quite compact and there were loads of them. I called the rabbits over as they seem to know everything, especially Tom. So I asked Tom who or what had made these markings in the snow, as I'd never seen them before.

"Oh, that's easy," said Tom in his deep voice, straightening himself up so he looked taller and giving the impression of importance. "They belong to the deer."

"Deer?" I asked. "What do they look like?"

"Well, if you care to turn around, you'll be able to see us," said this voice of authority.

So I did as I was told and turned around and there were three elegant brown creatures with four very long legs, staring back at me with the most beautiful big brown eyes, their long eyelashes slowly opening and closing at me.

"Hello," I said. "I'm Tuxedo. I'm a horse from Argentina."

"Oh, that sounds very grand," said one of the deer. She had a silky, soft voice. "I'm Charlotte, this is my friend Jessica and our friend Jeremy."

With that, they all stepped forward and slightly bowed their heads.

Jeremy introduced himself, in an "I'm in charge" sort of voice. "I'm the man of the herd. Well, I will be one day, but we are the best of friends," he said, turning to the girls.

Jessica just nodded and took a couple of steps back.

"She's a little shy," explained Jeremy.

"How did you guys get into my field? You need to open the gate," I asked, a little puzzled.

"We jumped it," said Jeremy in a Mr Boss-man voice.

"You jumped it? But that's impossible, it's so high." I didn't quite believe them.

"Yes, we did," said Charlotte. "Our back legs are like springs." All three of them then sank back onto their back legs and jumped back over the fence to show me. They made it look so easy and they could jump really high.

With that, they turned around, ran across my field and jumped over the fence to make their way back across the valley, hardly making a noise. I thought if Mercy and I tried to do that, we'd sound like a herd of elephants coming across the fields, not quiet at all.

 I shouted after them, "It was nice to meet you, hopefully see you again soon."

"Oh, you will," said Jeremy, "but you might not recognise me next time." I thought this was a very odd thing to say, so I shook my head and started to find some grass to nibble on, which was a bit hard as it was still covered with all this white stuff.

Then Mercy appeared in his field, so I trotted over to see him and to tell him of the new friends I'd met that morning. However, before I could, Mercy had rolled in the snow and wanted to play with this new toy, so we both started rolling, enjoying the different sensation it gave. What a great way to start the day. While playing in the snow that had covered our fields so thickly first thing, it was now beginning to melt, allowing the grass to be seen underneath. We then noticed the snowdrops starting to pop their little heads through.

Snowdrops are, as the name suggests, delicate white flowers that look like drops of snow. They are the first flowers of the year. Each month Mother Nature surprises us with different coloured plants, announcing the arrival of the months and seasons as we go through the year.

After playing in the snow for most of the morning, I was beginning to get a little bit cold and tired, so I was very pleased to see Mum coming back up to bring me in a little earlier than usual.

As we were walking back to the stables, I realised that Uncle Rick was here. Uncle Rick is my favourite farrier. A farrier is the person who takes the old shoes off and puts the new shoes on our hoofs. It's very important that the new shoes fit correctly, otherwise it can be very painful. Like when you have shoes that are a little too small, they pinch, so it's uncomfortable when you walk.

Uncle Rick is very gentle with me. So I have a relaxing hour while he re-shoes me. I have my shoes replaced every five weeks as my hoofs continually grow, just as your toe and fingernails do.

Mum gives me some fresh hay to keep me occupied, in case I get bored or fancy something to munch on. The first thing Uncle Rick does is remove my old shoes. Then he files my hoofs down a little where they have grown and fits me for the new shoe. He works on one shoe at a time, which means I have to stand on only three legs while he does this. It's a good job I have good balance.

After he's finished my manicure and pedicure, I feel ready to trot. So Mum gives me a groom and puts a dry and clean rug on me and we go for our potter for our quality time together in the snow. Walking in the snow is beautiful; everything is quiet and it feels so peaceful as we walk through the woods, leaving only our hoof- and footprints behind. What a perfect way to end a beautiful day.

Little Pearl of Wisdom for February

To make a new friend, and smile and say good morning to them, will definitely make their day.

You never know, they may become your best friend in the whole wide world.

Have fun in the snow, build a snowman and enjoy its beauty, as it only lasts for a short time. However, wrap up warm as you will get cold.

March

Howard the Hare and primroses

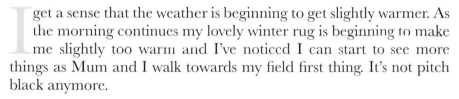

I get a sense that the weather is beginning to get slightly warmer. As the morning continues my lovely winter rug is beginning to make me slightly too warm and I've noticed I can start to see more things as Mum and I walk towards my field first thing. It's not pitch black anymore.

I have the best stable in the yard. It looks straight out towards my other horse friends so we can chat as well as look after each other. The other good point is that it looks straight down the road everyone enters by. I know the sound of Mum's car very well, so as soon as I hear it coming I put my head out of the top of my stable door to say good morning by neighing very loudly while shaking my head up and down. As I've said before, this is one of my favourite times of the day; the other is at the end of the day – which I'll explain later.

So after our morning cuddles and carrot kisses, Mum takes off my thick rug, gives me a quick brush down and up to the field we go. Without the rug I feel a little cold, but I know as soon as the morning gets brighter and the sun comes up I will get a lot warmer.

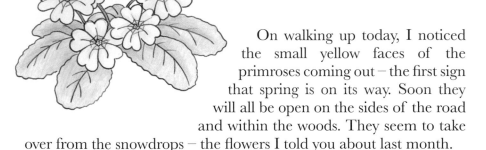

On walking up today, I noticed the small yellow faces of the primroses coming out – the first sign that spring is on its way. Soon they will all be open on the sides of the road and within the woods. They seem to take over from the snowdrops – the flowers I told you about last month.

Being the first one out, I put my head down and started to eat the grass, which tasted extra sweet this morning as it had a light dew on it. (Dew is what makes the grass slightly damp at the start of each day.)

As I was nibbling away enjoying my breakfast in my own little world, I didn't hear Mercy and the rabbits come over for their morning gossip. I brought my neck up so I could stand up straight and say good morning, but the rabbits and Mercy suddenly sucked in their breath and stared at me with very wide eyes. I looked behind me to see if there was anything there and said, "What's the matter? I can't see anything."

Gina stuttered slightly and said, "It's you, Tuxedo, it's your scars. We've never seen them before as you always have a rug on. They look so ugly, especially the big one on your chest. What happened to you?" Mercy and the rabbits all asked at the same time. "It's just we didn't know you had them, and so many."

"Well," I explained, "I had a horrible illness, but Mum got this very special medicine that would only cure me and I got better, but the illness unfortunately left me with these scars."

"Do they hurt?" asked Patsy in a concerned voice. She was still quite scared because they looked so ugly and frightening to her; even Tom hopped back slightly.

"No, they don't hurt," I said. "Do you find me frightening?"

"No," they all said together. "We love you, Tuxedo; we just weren't prepared for them, as we've never seen them before."

"I forget I've got them, they are part of my life adventures so far, and therefore part of who I am. Mum says it's important that you see the person that's inside, not what they look like on the outside or what possessions they may have."

"We don't care what you look like," said Gina. "The scars are part of your life and what you've been through so you should be proud of yourself, Tuxedo." With this, they all agreed and went about pottering around the fields, enjoying the sweet grass as they went.

But tranquillity was short-lived because Patsy then jumped so high and hopped as fast as her legs would allow her to reach the top of the field; all you could see was a little white tail bopping up and down very quickly. When she had reached us, she was out of breath trying to get the oxygen back into her lungs so she could talk.

Breathing in and out very fast and gasping for air, she said, "Footprints, large, like, like a rabbit, like us but too big to be ours." She was trying to get her breath back and finding it hard to string a sentence together, with only the important words coming out. We told Patsy to rest and relax and that I'd go and investigate. I must admit I was slightly nervous, but also inquisitive at the same time as I didn't know what I'd find.

So treading carefully, not wanting to ruin the unknown footprints, I set off to the bottom of my field to investigate. Treading carefully is not easy when you weigh half a tonne and you have four hoofs that are not dainty at the best of times.

Patsy was right: they were the biggest rabbit footprints I had ever seen. I was astounded. Who had such big feet? So I called over to Gina, Tom and Mercy, "You have to come and look at these because they certainly don't belong to me and they don't belong to any of you rabbits."

As they came over they were as surprised as I was; then Tom put his paw into the footprint and we started laughing as his footprint was tiny compared to this other one that looked like a dinosaur's.

As we were laughing a very deep voice said, "And what makes my footprint so funny?" We all turned around to see the tallest of ears we'd ever seen; they were giant, along with two very large brown eyes giving us a questioning look. We all opened our mouths to say something, but nothing came out, so Big Ears, which we later nicknamed him, introduced himself.

"I'm Howard, and I'm a hare. We are

related to you rabbits, but we don't have burrows. As you can see we are much bigger and faster than you."

"Mmm, we'll see about that," Tom muttered under his breath.

"Why haven't we seen you before?" I asked.

Howard replied, "Because we are very shy creatures and only come to very special places we feel safe in."

"So what's the difference between you and us?" asked Patsy, as she had now regained her breath and was not quite so frightened of Howard.

"Well, there are a few important differences. We are larger and faster, have longer ears and feet. When you rabbits are born, you are blind and hairless, whereas us hares can see and have fur. You live in burrows underground; we live in nests above the ground."

"Oh, there are a few differences," said Patsy. "I didn't realise."

"That's OK," said Howard, "but we are from the same family, so we can still be friends." He wiggled his large ears as he said it. "Anyway, I must go, I've got places to go and people to see."

"It was lovely meeting you," I said. "Let me introduce all of us to you. I'm Tuxedo, this is Mercy, we are the horses, and Tom, Gina and Patsy are the rabbits."

"Will we see you again?" asked Patsy, who had decided that Howard was quite gorgeous.

"You will. I'm here at dawn and dusk. I'll catch you later. Have a great day."

And he was right: hares are very fast, gone in a flash and across the field.

"Well, that's been another interesting morning," I said. "I hope the rest of the day will be a lot more relaxing." With that the sun came out and it felt lovely on my coat. The rabbits dozed in the sun and Mercy and I went back to the important task of nibbling on our sweet-tasting grass.

 Little Pearl of Wisdom for March

Don't judge a book by its cover.

Meaning that everyone is beautiful on the inside, no matter what colour, creed or size. We all have our differences in looks but we are from the same family. Everyone needs to be loved and have friends; otherwise it can be very lonely.

Look out for the different coloured flowers and the bright green leaves appearing on the trees, announcing the arrival of spring.

And if you are very lucky you'll see Howard.

April

Lambs, candle trees
April showers and rainbows

Again a lovely morning, it's getting a lot lighter these days. The sun now wakes me up earlier as it rises and shines in my face. Starting my day feeling her warmth on me, how nice is that? I've also noticed that the trees that line the driveway up to the yard are now full of bright green leaves and things that look like white candles on top. I must find out what they are as they look quite delicate.

As I was looking out of my stable door, enjoying the sounds of the morning chorus, my new friend Tabatha the Blackbird flew over for our morning chat. Standing there, watching the birds flying backwards and forwards while the other horses were poking their heads over their stable doors to say good morning to each other, I had a feeling of true contentment.

"This part of the day is very busy for us birds," explained Tabatha. "Firstly, we catch up with each other to find out what's been going on, then we go about collecting bits of branches, grass and moss to build our nests, getting ready to lay our eggs for this year's new family."

Tabatha was right, the girls were excitedly chirping to each other

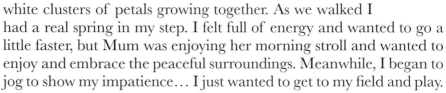

nine to the dozen, swapping gossip and telling each other where to go for the best twigs and moss to help build their nests. I then heard a familiar sound and it was Mum arriving.

We had lots of neck cuddles today, so we spent a little more time together than usual. She took my pyjama rug off and we pottered up to my field. When we passed under the candle tree, I looked up to get a closer look at the flowers, which are small white clusters of petals growing together. As we walked I had a real spring in my step. I felt full of energy and wanted to go a little faster, but Mum was enjoying her morning stroll and wanted to enjoy and embrace the peaceful surroundings. Meanwhile, I began to jog to show my impatience… I just wanted to get to my field and play.

Once there and with my head collar off, I cantered away bucking and snorting as I went, just so happy to be out in the warm sunshine. Spring was definitely here. As I was playing around, Tom, Gina and Patsy joined in, so we ended up playing a game of tag between us. By the time Mercy arrived we were all worn out as we'd been running around the field as fast as Ferraris.

"What have you guys been up to? You're all out of breath," asked Mercy.

In between breaths, Patsy explained that they'd been playing tag with me. "The only problem with that," she said, "Tuxedo has a very long stride compared to us and he also turns very quickly. We can't keep up with him."

"That's from when I was younger; we used to play a game called polo, where we had to turn very quickly and chase a ball."

"That sounds very tiring," said Gina.

"It was," I replied, "and not so great for my joints either."

"Well," said Tom, "have you guys seen the new addition to the fields?"

We all looked at each other, shook our heads and replied, "No, we haven't seen anything."

"Well," explained Tom (he liked starting conversations with "well") in his I'm-so-important voice, "they're like white balls of cotton wool, with four black thin legs and very big black eyes and they sort of jump all over the place, closely following their mums everywhere. They also make this bleating noise, which doesn't stop." With that Tom tried to mimic the noise, which made us all laugh, as it sounded like Tom had something stuck in his throat.

After Tom's in-depth description of these new things, we were all very inquisitive.

So off we pottered, the rabbits, Mercy and I. On our way we bumped into Howard the Hare again. We didn't see him at first, he was crouched down so low in the grass. "Good morning, everyone," he said as he pulled himself up, his big ears twitching. "Where are you all going?"

"We are going to see what the jumping white cotton balls are," said Mercy.

With that Howard started to laugh, making his big ears wiggle backwards and forwards even more, which looked quite odd.

"They're not cotton-wool balls, they're baby lambs," he said, "and they are so, so cute. Come, follow me, I'll introduce you to some of their mums who I know really well. The lambs are very friendly and inquisitive and will ask you lots of questions, sometimes all talking at the same time. We had better make a move quickly though as those black clouds behind us are promising to bring us some rain."

Patsy was very pleased to see Howard again as she had decided she had a slight crush on him, so she blushed slightly, saying it was nice to see him again.

Following Howard across his field, he took off so fast, forgetting we were behind him. We ran across the field, up the hill, back across another field, across the stream and then back up another hill. We had to stop then, as we were all huffing and puffing trying to keep up with him. Mercy asked between breaths if we were nearly there yet. Howard replied saying that the lambs were just around the corner and sure enough, a few more steps and there they were close to their mums.

Once we got there I recognised one of the sheep. It was Betsy. "Hello, Betsy, I haven't seen you for a while, how are you?"

Betsy turned around with a smile on her face. "Hello, Tuxedo, you look really well, how lovely to see you again. Hello, Howard, who have you brought with you?"

"These are Tuxedo's friends." With this he introduced the rabbits and Mercy to Betsy.

"Well, any friends of Tuxedo's are always more than welcome over this part of the estate. I've been rather busy since I last saw you, Tuxedo," explained Betsy. "I'm a mum now. Come over and meet my two children. This is Lily and this is Lola."

They both came bounding over, as their mum called them to say hello to everybody. They were very excited to meet us all, and Howard was right: they did speak at the same time, jumping up and down making bleating noises. They looked so cute. We also got to meet the rest of the flock. There were hundreds of mums, all with their young lambs, the mums enjoying nibbling on the grass, while the lambs were playing around in the spring sunshine.

As we were chatting away, we started to feel a few drops of rain, which were coming from the black clouds we'd run away from earlier.

"Here comes an April shower," said Patsy, "but it won't last for long, so we shouldn't get too wet." She was right. The shower lasted all of two minutes and then an amazing thing happened: a rainbow appeared. It was beautiful. If you have never seen one, then the next time it rains and the sun comes out at the same time, look out for it.

It's half a circle spanning from one field to another and it has these amazing cheerful colours – there are reds, oranges, yellows, greens, blues, indigos and violets. It always gives me a happy feeling when I see one. As we all looked up to enjoy the rainbow, we agreed it had again been another magical morning together.

 ### Little Pearl of Wisdom for April

Introduce your friends to others, enjoy the outdoors whatever the weather, and remember to look out for the rainbow, it's a happy feeling moment – and when you do see one, make a wish.

May

Meeting Picasso
exercise, wild garlic, bluebells and badgers

A couple of weeks ago it was time for me to change fields, as I didn't have much grass left in my winter one. So Mum and I made our way down to my summer field. It's a little further away from the stables with a semi-steep hill down to it, which means there is also a steep hill to climb back up when we go riding. I'll explain that later.

My summer field, however, is just perfect, opposite the woods where, at the moment, there is a carpet of blue. First time I saw it I was very surprised; it looked just stunning. Gina explained that it is the bluebell wood, named after these tiny blue flowers that grow very close together and have a very delicate scent, which only lasts for around three weeks. They are one of the main flowers that welcome late spring. The delicate perfume from the woods, along with the floor becoming a carpet of blue, it is just a beautiful sight; with the sun shining through it is a magical moment. The first thing I do in the mornings is to sniff the air for the delicate scent of these amazing flowers, as they are only around for a short time.

I really am very lucky as, apart from the woods, I also have stunning views across the 40-acre field with the hills in the background. The 40-acre field, I have to say, is one of my favourite places. This is where we go cantering; for us horses this is where we can run very fast for a long time, so it's like being in the school playground running around with your friends laughing and having fun and that is a fantastic feeling. Another bonus: the grass in my summer field is very sweet, lush and succulent. It's like having lots and lots of your favourite ice cream, and the best thing about it is you can eat as much as you like and you won't get told off.

A couple of friends I met last year came out of the woods to welcome me back. I haven't seen them for ages as I've been in my winter field; they were the pheasants Picasso and Samantha. They were both looking slightly slimmer than the last time I'd seen them, but I'm sure that was because they hadn't been able to pinch some of my daily dinner. He was named Picasso due to his amazing colouring, as his mum thought his colouring could have been designed and painted by the famous abstract artist himself.

"So who was Picasso?" I hear you asking. Well, his full name was Pablo Picasso. He was a Spanish artist who experimented with different painting techniques, painting objects in bright colours and not how you would normally see them. He would paint the arms where the legs should be and paint an object upside down. At the

time some people thought he was crazy, but he wasn't. Some of his paintings today are some of the most famous pieces of art in the world. His use of colours was amazing, some you would not normally put together. So that is why Picasso's mum called him after this famous painter. With his vibrant colours in his tail and coat, along with his red mask on his face and the little white collar around his neck, he always looks so stylish.

"Tuxedo, it's always nice to see you back down here again with us," said Samantha in her velvety, soft voice. "We have missed you. In fact, we bumped into Jeremy and the girls yesterday and he was saying that you should be moving down soon. Jeremy looks quite magnificent at the moment," she added.

That sounds intriguing, I thought.

I love being back in my summer field as this is when I get to stay out all day and night, that's a whole 24 hours. That's what you call a sleepover…

I don't go back into my stable in the evening now for a few months. Not until the cold nights start to return, which aren't until after the summer months. It feels quite grown-up being outside all the time. Some of the horses get a little frightened at night, due to the strange noises coming from the woods. So when dusk started to fall I called them all over and explained the different sounds and who they all belong to, so they would feel safer in their new surroundings, which is very important if you don't know what the strange noises are.

Firstly, I explained that it was Oscar the Owl who makes the twit-to-woo sound. He has a very important job, he is the night security guard for the woods. He can hear and see everything due to his big round eyes and he can turn his head nearly all the way around.

"Oh, wow!" said Mercy, trying to turn his head all the way round, straining himself and failing to do it. "That's just amazing."

"Oscar will look after us and pre-warn us if there is any approaching danger. He is also the encyclopaedia on all things wise, so if you have any questions, he will more than likely have the answer for you. The other sounds are either from the deer or the badgers walking across the floor of the wood, stepping on the leaves and twigs, making cracking noises as they go."

With this Mercy asked, "We know the deer, Jeremy, Charlotte and Jessica, but who and what are the badgers?"

"They're quite shy," I said. "They only come out at night, as they sleep all day in their burrows, which are underground. They are extremely gentle."

"But what do they look like?" asked Mercy, who was beginning to get impatient, as he didn't like it when others knew something he didn't.

They have black and white stripes down their faces and foreheads, which make them look like they are wearing masks. It's quite a striking look. Their dark grey bodies are short with dumpy legs. Their paws are big with long claws, which they use for hunting and making their burrows underground.

"The information talk is now over," I said. I was beginning to get a little hungry and my tummy was rumbling, telling me it was time to get back to my grass, which was extremely tasty.

After I'd had my grass munch and eaten a tad too much, I felt slightly full so I decided to have my afternoon snooze. This is my little treat to myself, lying in the warm sun, listening to the soothing and relaxing background noises of the different birds and animals going about their daily business.

Later on in the afternoon Mum arrived for our daily ride. She calls it her "Tuxedo time". This is my other favourite part of the day. So off we went to walk back up the hill to the stables, where I was tied up and got ready.

It can take a while to get ready. Firstly, my hoofs get picked out to make sure there are no stones or mud stuck in them. If there is a stone in there if can be quite painful to walk on. Like when you get one in your shoe, it hurts, so you end up hobbling.

The best part of getting ready for our ride is being groomed, which is when Mum uses all the different brushes, brushing my coat in a circular action. The brushes with the harder bristles are used to get rid of the mud and dirt from my coat. The brushes with the softer bristles are to give my coat a real glossy shine, and finally she brushes my thick mane and tail. I always love being groomed and having that clean feeling; it also makes me look quite handsome.

After being groomed it was time for Mum to put on my tack. "What is tack?" I hear you asking. Tack is the saddle and bridle, allowing Mum to ride me securely and safely for her sake. Firstly, she puts on my saddle, which is held in place by the girth. The girth is a leather strap with buckles at either end. These get attached to the straps on each side of the saddle. This keeps the saddle secure and stops it slipping off. Next is the bridle; it goes over my head with the bit. The bit goes in my mouth; the bit has rings on either side where the reins go. The reins allow Mum to slow me down and to let me know whether to go left or right.

So with me groomed and all tacked up we are ready to go. Mum puts on her riding hat and we are off for our daily adventure together.

Today Mum decided we were going to potter around the estate, which I also love to do as it gives me a chance to see the wonderful rhododendrons, one of my favourite flowers for this time of year. As the weather becomes warmer their flowers open up, showing off their varied colours of pinks and reds; there are also lilac ones. Their blooms are quite large, so you can see them from quite a distance away. A real sign summer is around the corner.

As we were wandering through the woods I started to sniff a very peculiar smell. It certainly wasn't the sweet smell of the bluebells; in fact, it was quite hard to describe. Actually quite pungent, making me wriggle up my nose; in fact, I decided it really was quite smelly. I made a note to myself to ask Oscar what it was, as I knew he would definitely know.

After five minutes we had left the "smelly clearing", as I called it, and we reached the 40-acre field where we go cantering; this is just the best place to play. At first, I started to jog with all four of my legs, it's like going skipping.

You know when you are so happy and excited you start skipping for joy, and then you run. Well, it's the same for me. Mum knows that I get excited at this point so she asked me to go into a proper trot not the jig I was doing, which is a bit messy and uncomfortable for her. So once my trot was more controlled, Mum asked me to go into a slow canter. Oh, that feels so good, as I knew what was about to come. Mum asked me to go faster and weeeeee, we were off, cantering across the 40-acre field, a feeling of pure joy. The wind was in my face, the pounding noise of my hoofs on the field and the rhythm of Mum and me enjoying the feeling of freedom together, it was fantastic. After our canter we went into the heart of the wood, which is a little cooler, and where the ferns had started to grow. As we were making our way around the estate, I noticed that some of the ferns were becoming taller than me; I must tell Mercy about this when we get back.

Little Pearl of Wisdom for May

When we see someone in a situation that they are a little frightened of, go and re-assure them and see if you can answer any questions that may be bothering them and listen to what they may be worried about.

Run with your friends very fast across a field enjoying that feeling of acceleration, and lastly like Picasso, think outside the box. If you want to paint a blue circle with a pink dot in it, do it. Still ask others for advice, but be true to yourself.

June

Meadow flowers
meeting Simon the Bee and the noise coming from the Quiet Garden

"Mercy, I have to tell you when I was out riding the other day, and walking through the woods, I noticed that the ferns are now a lot taller than me. Can you believe that?" I said.

"That's because you're small," said Mercy.

"No I'm not; I'm just the right height for me. I wouldn't want to be any taller," I replied.

"I'm only joking, Tuxedo, you know I like to tease you, but it's always in a fun and friendly way," Mercy said as he was trying to talk and chomp his way through the grasses and daisies all at the same time.

"Thank you," I said, "and don't talk with your mouth full. It's not a good look and it's very rude."

Waiting for Mercy to finish chewing, I noticed some small round black and yellow fluffy things had started to reappear on some of the meadow flowers after their winter rest.

"As I was about to say," said Mercy, "I can't believe we are halfway through the year already, which means summer has arrived, bringing her warmer days and longer nights. You can't beat them."

Mercy was indeed telling the truth. Summer had to be the best season for us horses, not having to wear those heavy rugs anymore. Not standing in the thick mud with our bottoms to the cold winds, which whistle through our tails. The other great thing, it seems to stay light forever and we get to stay out all night enjoying the warmth of the evening air.

There is a problem with summer though: it's the flies and the midges, which can be very, very annoying and tiring. Next time you see us horses in our fields during the summer months, you'll notice we spend most of the day swishing our tails and shaking our heads to get rid of the flies and midges that are biting us. They are very annoying, I can tell you, as they just don't stop.

Because I'm dark they seem to be attracted to my colouring, more so than Mercy. Mercy has a different colouring to me; he's a chestnut, which means he's ginger all over including his mane and tail. So when the flies land on him they are much less annoying as they don't seem to bite him so much. Mercy says it's because they like my Argentinian blood.

So Mum has bought me a new fly rug and face mask. It means the flies land on the rug and not directly onto my coat, making them much less annoying. The rug and mask are made from a very fine mesh so they don't make me hot, with the mask being see-through. The only thing, it does make me look as if I'm in a fancy-dress competition and I understand that, but I have the last laugh as I don't spend all day stomping my hoofs or shaking my head. Makes for a much more enjoyable and relaxing day.

As we were munching on our grass, enjoying the warmth of the sun on our backs, I realised that I could hear a low buzzing noise so I followed to see where it was coming from. It was coming from the far end of my field. As I walked to the corner of my field where the meadow flowers grew, whilst admiring their summer colours, from the red poppies, white cow parsley, blue cornflowers along with the bright yellow buttercups, I started to hear a low buzzing sound. The nearer I got, the louder the buzzing noise was. Then I noticed the round fluffy black and yellow balls going from one flower to another, stopping and then moving on. I couldn't see how they were doing this as they didn't seem to have any legs.

So, I put my nostril close to a blue cornflower and took in a deep breath sniffing the flower to try and understand what these fluffy round balls were doing.

"Watch it, you overgrown vacuum cleaner! What do you think you are doing? I nearly stung you and that would have been very painful for you."

"Oh, I'm so sorry, I didn't mean to frighten you," I said as I took a step back, "but who are you and what are you doing?"

"I'm a bee and the job I do is very important. I collect pollen from the flowers. Now move out of my way as I'm extremely busy and I don't want to be interrupted by any more vacuum cleaners like you."

I took a few more steps back, as I didn't want to stand on him. "But I still don't understand what you do, or what your name is and why you need pollen. I've got so many questions to ask you."

I decided to take charge of the situation and introduced myself first.

"My name is Tuxedo and I'm a horse and this is my summer field where my grass grows. That's what I eat to keep me fit and healthy. I'm here till September and then I go back into my winter field, which is close to the stables up the hill."

"How do you do, Tuxedo. My name is Simon and your field is very nice. You have lots of lovely meadow flowers, which is what we need to collect the pollen. We move around using our wings, flapping them together very, very fast, which makes that buzzing sound. As we move from flower to flower, we help pollinate them, to help them grow and make new little flowers, which they couldn't have done on their own."

"So they really rely on you?" I said.

"Oh, definitely," replied Simon.

"We have a very important job — we are the industrial army of the plant world," he said, slightly puffing out his small stripy chest.

"I still don't understand what you need the pollen for and when you've collected it what you do with it all."

"We take the pollen back to our home, which is called a hive, and we make honey," explained Simon.

"What's honey?" I said, thinking there seemed to be more questions than answers. Where was Oscar the Owl when I needed him?

"You have tasted honey," explained Simon, "but without realising it. Go over to that clump of clover and nibble on the end of the pink flowers."

So, I did as I was told and it tasted so sweet as I was munching on it.

"Well, that's the first stage of the honey process; that's the pollen," Simon said. "It's very good for you, it's natural in sugar, which gives you lots of energy. This time of the year, you will see many of my friends, as you ride around the estate, buzzing around all the different flowers. We especially like the lavender field at the bottom of the 40-acre field. So make sure you come and say hello to us, Tuxedo."

"Oh, I will," I said. "I just need to remember to slow down at that point as I do have a tendency to go a little fast there."

"Yes, we have noticed you," buzzed Simon.

"It's been a really interesting morning and lovely meeting you," I said.

"I've enjoyed meeting you too, Tuxedo, and please be careful when you sniff the fragrances of the flowers, as I might be up one of them and I don't want to sting you out of defence as it will hurt."

"Oh, I won't do that, I promise," I said and off I trotted across to the other side of the field to tell Mercy all about my most amazing and informative morning.

Before I started to tell Mercy about my meeting with Simon I needed a drink of water. While I was drinking, I asked Mercy, "What's beyond those trees?"

"That's the Quiet Garden," replied Mercy.

With this I snorted and started to laugh, which made the water come down my nose.

"How can it be called the Quiet Garden, as sometimes it gets really noisy in there? Admittedly it does quieten down sometimes. Is there some sort of party going on that we are not invited to?"

"No, silly," replied Mercy. "That will be Georgina and Charles and their new baby goslings."

"Who are Georgina and Charles?" I asked.

"They are the parents of the goslings," said Mercy.

With that I stomped all four of my hoofs. "Mercy, don't be so difficult, you know what I mean. I've never heard a racket like it."

"OK, OK," said Mercy, "keep your rug on." He enjoyed joking

around with me. "They are called Canada Geese. They come here to have their young as it's a safe environment to bring them up, and when they are big and strong they move to more open areas like parkland and lakes."

"Are they from Canada?" I asked

"No," replied Mercy. "Initially they were, but they were introduced to Britain ages ago and have now made it their new home. Mind you, I don't know where Canada is."

"I do. It's north of America, as I remember being told when I was younger. I was from Argentina in South America. America is the bit in the middle when you look at a map. Then Canada is above America and right at the top is Alaska."

"How do you know all that?" asked Mercy.

"It's because I'm a well-travelled horse," I replied.

"It's always like having a mini geography lesson with you, Tuxedo. Wish I'd travelled as much as you," replied Mercy.

"In fact, wouldn't it be great to be able to fly like the geese? Our distant cousins the unicorns could. But let's not get sidetracked. Back to these geese, I'm intrigued."

With that, Georgina and Charles decided to bring their children out for a walk, to show them the world outside the Quiet Garden.

So after Georgina had checked all her children were clean, neat and tidy, Charles spoke to them. "OK, chaps, stand in one line behind each other and stop talking. You are about to meet some of the other animals that live on the estate, so make sure you smile and say good morning to all." With that he turned to his wife, Georgina, and said, "Ready, my dear, all in order, let us proceed."

The family ran forward for a few strides, starting to flap their wings and then they rose higher and higher, over the wall, over the trees and then into the open skies of the estate. They stretched their wings and started to fly and play in the warm pockets of air called thermals.

Mercy and I looked up to see them enjoying swooping and gaggling with each other. Georgina and Charles were having to work hard to keep up with their energetic children. One of the goslings thought it would be funny to glide low over our heads, which sent Mercy and me running across our fields as we were sure we could feel the tips of his wings on our ears. A little too close for comfort!

We stood there for a few moments watching the family having fun together in the openness of the sky above.

"Now," said Mercy, "what were you going to tell me about your morning?"

 Little Pearl of Wisdom for June

Realising the smallest of things and creatures around you can make a big difference to you and the world in general. So open your eyes wide and appreciate everything, sharing with others your new-gained knowledge.

And remember you are the right height for you.

Don't try to fly; leave that to the animals that have wings.

Teasing and joking around with your friends is fun, but remember never do it to be spiteful or hurtful to anyone.

Butterflies, moles
meeting Jeremy again

"July has to be the best month of the year." Gina yawned, as she stretched out on the long grass.

"I agree," said Patsy, as she sat up twitching her ears and stroking her nose with her paws. "The air just smells so sweet, you can really smell the lavender and the meadow flowers." With that, she took a deep breath in, sighed and lay back down again, as if everything was too much of an effort.

Tom then sat up and asked, "Did anybody feel the earth move around them last night?"

Patsy and Gina looked at each other, rolled their eyes, and replied, "No, Tom."

"Well, it can't have been just me," he said, in a don't-you-believe-me type voice. "Tuxedo, did you feel the earth move last night?"

At this point I was having my morning snooze, so I wasn't really listening. Cocking one ear back, I said, "Sorry, Tom, what did you say?"

"I said," said Tom in his now-I'm-annoyed voice because nobody seemed to be taking him seriously, "did you feel the earth move around you last night, Tuxedo?"

I thought for a minute. "Yes, I did feel some earth being flicked around me, but I couldn't see what it was or where it was coming from, so I decided to ignore it as it wasn't doing me any harm."

"Well, this is ridiculous," said Tom. "We need to get to the bottom of this."

I realised then I wasn't going to be allowed to continue my snooze, so I walked over to the rabbits.

"OK, what do you suggest," I said, "so we can all go back to what we were doing?"

Gina and Patsy agreed, as they wanted to go back to sunbathing themselves in the long grass.

"Right," said Tom, who also enjoyed being in charge. "I think as there are four of us, we should split into four groups and each of us goes to one corner of your field, explore what's there and then report back here on what we find, in around 20 minutes."

Everyone nodded, as that seemed an excellent plan. So off the rabbits hopped in their different directions and I pottered off to the corner I'd been allocated. When we met back in the middle of my field, it seemed that everyone had discovered the same thing – lots and lots of small triangular-shaped mounds of earth.

Tom was very happy about this, as it meant they would now start taking him seriously. "We have to know what's going on," he said.

"Most definitely," I said, as I was now getting worried that something was making my grass disappear and I didn't know what it was.

As we were pondering on what it could be, suddenly, these three figures jumped out of the woods. We were all so frightened we forgot about the mounds of earth. We turned around and screamed as there were the deer, Charlotte, Jessica and Jeremy. But that wasn't the problem; the scary thing was that Jeremy seemed to have a tree actually growing out of his head.

"What on earth is the matter?" said Jeremy in a voice that had grown deeper and louder.

"It's you," I said. "Do you know how frightening you look? You have branches coming out of the top of your head, that's not normal."

"It is normal for us male deer," said Jeremy, extending his neck out and in doing so making himself look even taller. "These are my antlers; look how magnificent they are." As he turned around you could see they did look very splendid indeed. "I'm turning into an adult."

"Is that why your voice is a little deeper?" asked Gina, who secretly thought Jeremy was quite gorgeous.

"Yes," said Jeremy. "I'm becoming a grown-up, as I have to start protecting Charlotte and Jessica."

"He's also becoming very bossy," said Charlotte, "telling us what to do all the time."

With that Jessica agreed, which surprised everybody, as normally she hardly spoke.

"Well, you're still very handsome," said Gina, and she blushed slightly, so to disguise her embarrassment she pretended she had an itchy nose.

"Well, it's lovely to see you again," I said, "and you all look very well."

"So do you," said Charlotte. "Looks like you've put on a little weight since we last saw you in February. Your rug is a little tight around your tummy."

"I know, this is my old summer rug, my new one is in the wash. I've had this one for years. Can you believe it; it used to be too big for me when I first got it. I was so skinny then. Thinking back, I also felt tired and sleepy most of the time. But now I've put on weight and am eating healthily, my energy levels have improved and I feel the best I have ever been. I know I'm getting a new summer rug soon, as Mum measured me up for one the other day."

"Well, anyway, enough of this small talk," said Tom, turning to the deer and slightly bowing, which made Gina and Patsy roll their eyes even more. "Jeremy and ladies, we seem to have a problem. Tuxedo's field is being dug up by something or someone, as there are mounds of earth everywhere. Mind you, they are very tidy mounds of earth, all in triangle shapes."

"Undoubtedly, that's the moles," said Charlotte. "They are just so cute, but you hardly see them as they work at night and are quite shy creatures, but once you get to know them they are very friendly."

"Really?" I said. "The rate they are going in my field, it's beginning to look like it's been ploughed ready for sowing wheat or something." With that, everybody started to laugh, seeing the worried look on my face, as I thought my whole field of grass was going to disappear.

"You'll be fine," said Jeremy. "They don't dig up that much and look how big your field is."

"I suppose," I said, "but why do they do it at all? I'm going to go and find Oscar to get an answer to my question. What are you guys up to for the rest of the day?" I asked.

"We're going back into the woods," replied Jeremy, "as it's cooler for us in there, but we'll see you around."

"Next time I see the head mole, I'll speak to him," said Charlotte, "so you can meet him."

"That would be great," I said, as I was still slightly worried that all my grass was going to disappear overnight.

So, after everyone had disappeared for their afternoon naps, I decided to go and visit Oscar to get the answers to my many questions about the moles. I had to go into the woods, as that is where he lives.

I stood under his tree. "Oscar, are you there? Sorry to disturb you, but I'm a little worried about the moles digging up my field. I've never seen them, but Charlotte said they are initially quite shy, but are friendly once they get to know you. I just need to know what they are doing and are they going to leave me any grass?"

Oscar popped his head out from behind his little house in the tree. "Hello, Tuxedo, you must be very concerned to come and see me, but you don't need to be. The moles won't dig up your entire field. In fact, they've probably moved on to another field already. Charlotte is right: you hardly ever see them as they spend most of their lives underground. They are around 6 inches long, with very soft fur and huge spade-like front paws, which are what they use for digging. They dig around 20 metres of a tunnel a day. The earth you see on top of your field is the earth they excavated underneath the grass to build their tunnel. While they are digging they are eating the grubs and earthworms, which are part of their diet."

"So they are not eating my grass?" I asked.

"No," said Oscar. "The soil has just been placed on top of it. Your grass is still there, Tuxedo. In fact, they are doing you a favour. They are making the earth healthier by aerating it, which means your grass next year will taste even sweeter."

"Oh, I feel much happier now you've explained it. Thank you so much, Oscar. I'll wander back to enjoy the rest of my snooze. I was quite distressed."

"Where have you been?" asked the rabbits, hopping out of the woods as soon as they saw me with their tails bobbing up and down.

"I've been to see Oscar, who has explained the moles to me."

"So are they making your grass disappear?" asked Gina.

"No, not at all. In fact, they are improving it for me. I'll tell you about it later. But I'm on my way back to have a rest, as I'm quite tired now."

Just as I was drifting off, and dreaming of acres and acres of lush green grass without any mounds of earth in it, I felt a very light, gentle touch against my ear. It then stopped and touched the other

ear and stopped again. It was a very delicate sensation; I
thought maybe I was dreaming it. But then I felt it on
my neck and then on the tip of my nose. So, I
opened my eyes to see what it was. I looked
down my nose, which made me go a little
cross-eyed. What I could see were very
colourful petals that looked like
they had come from a flower.
Still on the end of my nose, it
seemed to open and close, then
stayed open showing its colourful
petals to the sun.

It did this a few times and it was tickling my
nose, so I knew I was about to sneeze. So as not to frighten it, I
whispered, "Excuse me," in my quietest voice. "I think I'm going to
sneeze, as you're tickling the hairs on my nostrils, and I don't want to
frighten or hurt you."

"Hello, I'm Edward, I'm a butterfly. I'll just fly onto this flower in
front of you, so you can see me and we can have a proper chat. My
wife will be joining me soon, so you'll be able to meet her too."

"That would be lovely," I replied. "I don't think I've ever seen
anyone as colourful or as beautiful as you."

"Yes," replied Edward, opening and closing his wings. "They are
quite lovely. I'm a Red Admiral butterfly; our markings are quite bold,
with striking red bands on each wing with white dots on the top."

"Yes, and I've got similar markings," said a little voice who had
landed on the flower next to Edward.

"Ah, this is my lovely wife, Emily," said Edward.

"Pleased to meet you, Emily and Edward. I'm Tuxedo. The colours on your wings are just stunning," I said.

"Thank you," said Emily, fluttering them in the sunshine. "We are not the only types of butterflies you'll see over the next few weeks. There are quite a few of us, all with different colourful markings. When you pass the purple plant, which is the buddleia, you'll see a few of us there. It tends to be our meeting place."

"I look forward to that; it's been lovely meeting you both," I said, and with that they flew off and followed each other from flower to flower, both looking graceful and happy being in each other's company.

As I'd been out in the sun for most of the day, I walked over to get some water. "Wow, what a day," I said to Mercy, who was also enjoying a drink.

"You always have exciting days, Tuxedo. You make sure you get the most out of each one," replied Mercy.

"I think it's very important, there's so much to see and to learn about." With that I looked up, as I heard some familiar footsteps. It was Mum, walking down the hill. She had a big bag with her and I was sure I could smell carrots wafting down on the light breeze.

Mum came into my field, giving me a hug, and took off my old tight summer rug. I badly needed to scratch as I was very itchy, so I cantered away for a few paces, and then got down onto the grass and rolled a few times.

Ahh, that felt so much better, shaking myself as I got back up and trotting back to Mum to check my presents out.

First, she gave me a quick groom to get rid of the grass and mud I'd picked up while rolling, giving me a back scratch as she used one of the harder brushes, then she opened the big present, which was my new summer rug. It fitted perfectly. It's very white so you can see me from afar, but it covers everywhere including my tummy. The only things not covered are below my knees and my face. To deal with this she's bought me a new fly mask as well, so the flies won't be able to get into my eyes, which definitely means they won't be annoying me anymore. And, I was right; she also had my favourite – carrots.

Little Pearl of Wisdom for July

There is always an explanation for the strangest of things. Keep asking questions until you have the correct answer.

Next time you see a deer with antlers, look how magnificent he is, it could be Jeremy.

With the butterflies, look how pretty they are. If you can plant a butterfly-friendly plant in your garden, they will come and say hello to you.

August

Streams, monsters
being washed and the night sky

"These summer days are just fantastic!" I said to Mercy, as we were having our morning catch-up across the fence. The sun now rises very early, ready for the start of her new day, and doesn't go down until much later, making the evenings much longer. In fact it's not dark for very long at all now.

"More time to eat even more grass," said Mercy, who indeed seemed to eat all day long non-stop. At least I do stop eating when I feel full, otherwise I think I might pop. As we were contemplating the lightness of the days, we became aware of a humming noise, which seemed to be getting nearer.

We couldn't see anything, but a noise was certainly there. It was coming nearer and then it seemed to go away again. We decided there was no point in investigating it, as firstly, we couldn't see what it was and secondly, it wasn't doing us any harm.

As Mercy continued eating, I decided to lie down and have a snooze, as I had been awake most of the night looking at the night sky. The next time you see a clear sky in the evening, make a note to yourself, when it gets really dark, to go outside with your family

and friends to enjoy seeing the moon and stars together. It looks like lots and lots of glitter has been sprinkled everywhere. Last night the stars were so bright, it was as if you could touch them. All twinkling, saying hello; it was really magical.

The morning was quite uneventful as it was very hot, so the deer and the rabbits had decided to stay in the woods, where it was a lot cooler. The butterflies were going from flower to flower following the bees, who seemed to be slightly in front of them all the time, even though it wasn't a race.

As it began to cool down, I could hear Mum's footsteps coming down the hill. I was really pleased to see her, so I neighed to say hello and trotted over, giving her a nuzzle to show in my horsey way how much I loved her.

She took off my summer rug and put my head collar on to lead me up the hill to the stables. This meant we were going for our daily ride. I love going for my rides with Mum. This is where we change our speeds going from fast to slow at different places as we explore the estate together. On our way back to the stables we saw Betsy with Lily and Lola.

Lily and Lola came running over. "Hi, Tuxedo," they said in unison.

"Hello," I said. "My, you two have grown since I last saw you."

"They certainly have," replied Betsy, "and they're not running and jumping up and down and being a nuisance, which makes for a more peaceful day."

"Ah, but we were younger then," said Lily, "and had a lot of energy to burn off and everything was exciting and it all had to be investigated."

"And investigate you did," said Betsy.

"So where are you off to, Tuxedo?" asked Lola.

"Mum and I are off for our afternoon ride," I replied.

"Enjoy," they all said. "Tell us about it, when you get back."

When we got to the stables, Mum groomed me, which as you know I just love being pampered. So after she was happy that I looked presentable, on went my saddle and bridle. Mum put her hat on and off we set.

Down we went through the woods, which were lovely and cool, so I totally understood why some of the animals come here to get out of the heat of the day.

We walked through the stream, which felt refreshing and cool against my legs, climbing up the bank on the other side to get us back onto the track, which takes us around the estate.

As we were approaching the hill, Mum asked me for a canter, which I did no problem, as I love going fast, as you know. As we got to the top we slowed down and I started to hear the noise Mercy and I had heard earlier in the morning. Except this time, it was beginning to get

a little louder. I felt a little scared, I must admit, as we reached the top of the hill, as I didn't know what we were going to find.

Mum seemed not to be worried or frightened, so I thought, Well, it can't be anything too dangerous, as I really trust her and know she would not put me in any danger. As we went through the opening onto the 40-acre field, I was stunned and shocked, so much so that I couldn't move any of my hoofs; they felt like they were glued to the ground.

Let me explain. When we normally come through the clearing from the woods onto the 40-acre field, all you can see for miles and miles is lots of lovely long grass. But today all I could see was big square shapes everywhere and now the grass was very, very short as if it had had a severe haircut and there was that noise again. But this time I could see what it was: it was a grass-eating monster machine. It swallowed up as much grass as possible in its mouth. I'd never seen anything like it before, it ate so much grass. More than Mercy! Then at the back end of the machine it spat the grass out into huge square shapes, which is what I'd seen when we came through the clearing.

Mum asked me to walk forward, which I did, but very slowly in case these big grass squares were going to run and attack me. So, as we approached the first one I edged forward slightly and sniffed it. The first thing I noticed was that it smelt so sweet and I recognised the smell but couldn't quite remember where I'd smelt it before. I tried to nibble on it, but Mum pulled me back before I could get a sneaky bite.

Once I'd realised that these strange square objects weren't going to hurt me, I relaxed. So we rode across the 40-acre field, avoiding the grass-eating monster, who by now was a safe distance away.

The rest of the ride was brilliant, full of fun, running until I was a little out of breath. So we then slowed down and walked back through the stream, into the woods where the afternoon sun was coming through the trees bathing everything in a golden light. We made our way back to the stables leisurely, savouring this bit of the afternoon.

When Mum took off my saddle and bridle, I was very hot and sweaty. As it was still a warm afternoon Mum decided to wash me. I really, really love being hosed down; all the lovely-smelling soaps and shampoos are scrubbed and rubbed into my coat, tail and mane. Oh, I could stand there for hours being pampered.

Mum spends a lot of time on my mane and tail, which are both very thick and, as everyone tells me, two of my best features. But my mane is still quite itchy, so Mum has decided to cut it off so she can get the anti-itching cream closer to my skin, which would stop the irritation.

It should make a difference, as I hate being itchy.

After I'd been hosed down to get rid of the excess shampoo and soap I felt squeaky clean, and some of the birds that were flying around, catching midges for their dinner, all chirped to say how handsome I looked.

While I'm waiting to dry so I can get my mane cut, I'll take this time to explain why my mane and tail get so itchy this time of the year. It's caused by the flies and midges using them as their playground. Playing hide and seek is one of their favourite games, as they hide in my thick hair. Great fun for them, but not for me. The anti-itching cream has a smell that the flies and midges don't like, keeping them away, which means they don't use me as their amusement park to play their games.

While we were waiting for me to dry, Mum made herself a cup of tea and she gave me some hay to munch on. Now I recognised the smell from the hay was similar to the squares I'd just seen in the 40-acre field, I made a note to tell Mercy I now know where our hay comes from. So Mum and I enjoyed a relaxing few minutes together, both being content in our own little worlds, but enjoying the closeness of being together.

When I felt dry, I let Mum know by giving her a nudge and a kiss.

So she went to get the clippers, this is what she uses to cut my mane very short. It's called being hogged. She starts at the bottom of my mane and works up towards my ears. It's an odd sensation, quite tickly in places. The hair falls away and I feel so much lighter. With the mane removed, Mum then rubs my anti-itch medicine close to the skin where the mane was. This will heal any sores I might have and the midges and flies stay away.

Now I'd been all primped and cleaned, I couldn't wait to tell Mercy about what I'd found out on my ride.

Mum went to get my dinner to take with us and we started to walk back down the hill. As we passed Lily and Lola, they asked, "Did you have a good ride, Tuxedo? Wow, you look amazing, have you been washed? And you've had your mane cut off; it looks so much better."

"We had a great ride, thank you," I replied. "I saw the grass-eating monster machine, which I'll tell you about, and thank you for your compliments." I made a note to self to get washed more often.

When we reached my field, Mercy came trotting over, still with a mouth full of grass. "Have a good time?" he asked.

"I've got lots to tell you, but give me a minute," I replied.

Mum put my summer rug back on, filled up my water, gave me my dinner, and kissed me goodnight.

"Well," said Mercy, "tell me more." This time he actually had stopped eating.

"Can I eat my dinner first? I'm a bit hungry." My tummy was beginning to tell me to eat; it was rumbling.

"No, tell me first; you've been gone for ages," said Mercy, swishing his tail to get rid of the flies that were beginning to annoy him.

7

"Oh, all right then." So I stepped back from my dinner and suddenly Picasso and Samantha appeared. "Now wait, you two, I have to tell Mercy all about my adventure, including meeting the grass-eating monster machine and being hogged. So please both of you sit there and listen to my story and then we can enjoy my dinner together."

Little Pearl of Wisdom for August

To appreciate the night sky with the stars, planets and the different phases of the moon.

Enjoying having showers and baths using all the nice-smelling shampoos and soaps.

If something appears frightening tell somebody about it, so they can explain what it might be, so it won't frighten you anymore.

September

Exercise
nutrition and conkers

"Wow, that was such fun!" I said. My nostrils were flaring, tail high, with beads of sweat on my forehead.

"Oh, yes," replied Mercy, who unlike myself was out of breath. Gasping in and out to get the oxygen back into his lungs while trying to talk at the same time, he was beginning to think that playing tag with me wasn't such a great idea.

As we both looked around Auntie Karen, Mercy's mum, was standing in the field with her hands on her hips looking less than impressed with us both, as she was at this point soaking wet.

"I don't think at the moment we are in your mum's good books. She keeps shouting at us. I think I might take off again," I suggested.

"Oh no, don't do that," said Mercy. "I think we're in big trouble."

Now before we go any further, I think it's important that you know the background of this adventure.

It all started early this morning when the rain began to fall very heavily, the wind came up and then there was a loud clap of thunder.

Mercy became a little frightened and jumped over the tape into my field.

"Hello," I said. "This is fun, we've never been in the same field together."

"No," replied Mercy, "but I came over as I don't like being on my own in a thunderstorm."

"I'll look after you," I said, "and we can play." With that, the wind came up.

When Mercy had jumped over, he had managed to break the tape that separated our fields. So, as the wind got stronger it pulled the tape further away from its fasteners. Therefore, instead of having two small fields, we now had one huge one.

Now this had never happened before in all the years we'd been next door to each other in our winter or summer fields. So, the opportunity to be slightly naughty was too good to be missed. We agreed, for one morning only, we'd be naughty boys. Mercy was so excited he was already prancing around just thinking about it.

"Well, the game is called tag," I explained. "You run after me, and if you touch me on my bum, then you win and then it's my turn to catch you. The aim is you have to turn around as fast as possible without stopping and run full pelt to the other side of the field."

"That sounds like amazing fun," replied Mercy.

"OK, ready to catch me?" I said.

"I want to go first," said Mercy. "You know I used to be one of the country's finest racehorses. I know all about speed."

"All right," I replied. "Let's see what you're made of, but don't forget I'm a Criollo and I have speed and endurance."

So with that we played a serious game of tag. Now unbeknown to us, as we were in our own little worlds, running around like crazy, Mercy's mum, Auntie Karen, was walking down the hill to give Mercy his breakfast.

As she was on her way down the hill she noticed not only were we together in the same field, but we were running around like a couple of crazy horses.

Oh well, she thought. I'll catch Tuxedo first, as he's always a well-behaved boy, and then I'll tackle Mercy. Now this is where it all started to go horribly wrong.

Firstly, the heavens opened and it started to rain so heavily you couldn't see in front of you, never mind hear anything.

So, here we were running around chasing each other and Auntie Karen was calling to us both to stop playing and to settle down. At this point, she wasn't very impressed with the situation as she was now very wet, a little cold, and neither of us was listening or paying any attention to her.

With that, she then decided to come and catch me. Normally I would have stopped playing, walked over to her and bowed my head so she could put my head collar on. Now for some unknown reason I decided to be a rebel and took off in the other direction. With the rain in my face, I galloped to the other side of this now very big field, enjoying myself immensely. With that, Mercy followed me, so Auntie Karen had no hope of catching either of us.

We did this a few more times, but Mercy was by now beginning to get tired. Auntie Karen realised this and caught him first. He didn't want to be caught, as he knew he was going to get a telling off. Even though secretly he was pleased to stop; after running around with me for what seemed like ages, he was now quite exhausted.

In the meantime, I hadn't finished galloping around the field. I was having a great time. After a few more circles around the perimeter, I realised it wasn't as much fun on my own. So I stopped and turned around to see Mercy apologising to Auntie Karen for breaking the fence.

I thought I should own up too, so I walked over to her to apologise. She accepted our apologies and gave us both big hugs.

Auntie Karen led me back to my field while the fence was being repaired. Mercy went about having his breakfast.

Life returned to normal, but it had been a morning we would never forget.

After all that running around I began to feel a little tired, so decided on a midday nap before I caught up with the rest of my friends in the afternoon.

The first ones to arrive as normal were the rabbits and then Oscar flew in.

"You can certainly tell that the season is about to change," stated Oscar in his all-important owl voice.

"Oh, I agree," replied Tom, who was not one to miss out on an important conversation, especially with Oscar.

"The mornings and evenings are beginning to get darker slightly earlier each day and there is a slight chill in the air as well. I think summer is about to bid farewell to us until next year," explained Oscar.

"But it's been an amazing summer, so warm and hardly any rain, which means I've been out riding most days. What more could a horse wish for?" I said. "I've also noticed different things appearing on my recent rides, like all the different types of mushrooms growing from the floor of the wood, and there's this purple flower, very small but delicate, that grows near the moss.

"I must admit, I'll be glad when Mum changes me into my intermediate rug, as it's slightly thicker than the one I have on at the moment. I can certainly feel the drop in temperature at night; it can get a little chilly," I said.

"That's because of the clear nights we've been having," explained Oscar. "Not a cloud in the sky, which has a plus side: it means the night sky looks amazing with all the stars twinkling and with the full moon the other evening it was a beautiful sight.

"Be careful of those mushrooms, Tuxedo. Don't go eating them as some are poisonous, which could give you an upset tummy. The purple flower you saw is called heather; you see a lot of it on the moors of Scotland, which is a lot further up north from here and a lot colder," he added.

"Tuxedo, you have more rugs than I have…" Mercy said, looking around to see what he could say to finish off the sentence. He came up with, "…grass."

"Well, that's not hard," replied Howard the Hare as he hopped in. "You've eaten it all." With that, everyone fell about laughing. Every time you look at Mercy, he has a mouthful of grass.

"I like my grass," said Mercy, who went about finding and munching on some more.

"Hello, Howard," I said. "I haven't seen you for ages. Where have you been?"

"I've been lying low in the 40-acre field, but I've seen you quite a few times, Mr Tuxedo, cantering across the field and going quite fast, I may add."

"I know, I can't help it," I replied. "I just love the exercise; it makes me feel so good." With that, I did a little jig. "So what are you up to for the winter, Howard, now the 40-acre field is bald?"

"Bald?" said Gina. "Why, what has happened?"

"They've cut all the grass," I said. "That grass-eating monster has cut all the long grass and made square objects from it. It makes our hay, I think."

"That's not a monster," explained Oscar. "That's the hay-baling machine, which is how your hay is made. Which is what keeps the sheep and you horses in food during the winter months."

"You are very lucky," said Howard. "You will have noticed that the squirrels and the hedgehogs are on an eating mission at the moment."

"Yes, I've noticed that," replied Mercy. "They seem to be eating more than me. Why is that?" he asked, still lazily chewing on some grass.

"Well, unlike you horses, I may add," said Oscar, "you are very lucky. Most of the other animals don't have mums who make sure they get breakfast, lunch and dinner every day. They need to eat as much as possible, so they can store the fat in their bodies to keep them warm over the winter months while some of them sleep; this is called hibernation. The squirrels especially hide their food so the other animals can't find it."

"Like having their own secret store," said Patsy.

"Yes, that's right," replied Howard. "Because when it's cold, icy and the ground is covered in snow, it's very hard to find food, so they need to put it somewhere safe for when they need it."

"I remember when I was skinny, I always felt cold with hardly any energy. I also felt a little sad and lonely sometimes, so I understand how the fat in their bodies can keep them warm," I replied.

"Well, you should be roasting this winter, Tuxedo," said Mercy, "as you're not exactly skinny now and you've made lots of new friends too, so you'll never be lonely again."

"I've seen how much energy you have now," said Howard, "and sometimes there's a little too much, I may add."

I chose to ignore that comment.

"You do look very handsome," said Patsy, who still thought I was the best-looking horse she had even seen.

It's a good job I'm a dark-coloured horse, as I did blush slightly at her very kind compliment.

With that, we all had a good morning laugh together, agreeing that friendship is a very important thing, while Mercy and I were doing different horse poses, pretending to be models.

While we were larking around, Oscar had been thinking hard and announced out of nowhere, "I think more animals should realise how important it is to eat the correct foods. I mean only the other day I saw Lily and Lola eating the blackberries like mad. They are an excellent source of vitamin C, but too many will give you tummy ache."

Tom, who thought he knew everything, turned to Oscar. For as far as Tom was concerned, Oscar did know everything; he was the most intelligent owl in the world.

"What are vitamins and who's C?" he asked.

"That's a very good question, Tom," replied Oscar. "I will do my best to explain."

"Vitamins are found in all the foods we eat. Your body needs them to work properly and help you grow."

"The main vitamins are A, B, C and D. Vitamin A is found in carrots and helps you see in the dark. Vitamin B is found in grains; it helps your body to make energy from food. Vitamin C is found in fruits and helps to heal you when you cut yourself. Vitamin D is found in milk. It helps to make healthy bones."

"That explains why horses can see in the dark," said Gina, "as their mums are always giving them carrots."

"That's really interesting. I didn't realise how important the different vitamins are," said Tom. "Thank you, Oscar. I'll go and explain them to Lily and Lola so they understand the importance of how many berries they are eating. And what else they should eat to have a healthy and balanced diet." So off he hopped.

"Oscar, before you fly off, I've got a couple more questions to ask you that have been bugging me. Hopefully you have the answers for me," I said. "The first one is, a few months ago, in the clearing as you approach the 40-acre field, there was a unique smell; it only lasted a few weeks and I haven't smelt it since, which is a good thing as it was quite stinky. The other thing is, when we come back from our ride, I've noticed loads of brown shiny balls on the floor underneath the candle trees."

"They are easy questions to answer," replied Oscar. "The first one: the smell is from the wild garlic. They have white clusters of flowers and sometimes the rabbits will nibble on them, and you're right, they are only around for a few weeks, normally the same time as the bluebells. The other is, remember the candle tree you saw back in the spring? Well, the flowers that looked like white candles bore fruit, which in turn became conkers. The conkers are the shiny brown balls you see on the ground, but they are not safe for you to eat. The children that come to the stables love them, as they are a great source of entertainment as they are used to play the game of conkers, which goes back years. Has that answered your questions, Tuxedo?"

"Oh yes, makes more sense now. Thank you, Oscar. I'm glad you've cleared those up for me as they've been bothering me for a while," I replied.

"Time for some vitamin C, I think," said Mercy.

That seems like a very good idea, I thought.

Little Pearl of Wisdom for *September*

It's OK to be a little naughty for one day a year with your friends, but only for a little bit and nobody gets hurt.

Make sure you get an equal amount of all the vitamins you need to stay strong and healthy.

Enjoy playing conkers — get the really bright shiny ones.

October

Changing of the leaves
the mud incident and meeting Romeo

I woke up feeling great. I'd just had my first night's sleep back in my stable after being out in the summer fields. Even though I love my summer field and being out 24/7, there was something quite special about being back in my stable in the evening, all snuggled up. My bedding is made from soft wood shavings, which makes lying down very comfortable along with keeping me nice and warm away from the heavy winter rains and cold icy winds.

All the horses are now back in their stables for the evenings, so nobody is left outside to deal with the elements.

As I was in that dozing stage of not being quite awake but also not quite asleep, I heard the familiar sound of Mum's car coming down the lane.

I had a big yawn, stood up and shook myself, getting rid of any shavings that had stuck themselves to my coat and tail. All the other horses were still fast asleep as their mums came down later to put them out.

Mum came walking towards me whispering, as she didn't want to wake the others. "Good morning, my little man," she said, opening my stable door and coming in giving me my morning cuddle and carrots.

Mum then put on my thicker outdoor rug and, after I had given her some carrot kisses, we pottered off up to my winter field. My winter field is a lot closer to the stables with no hill to climb, making it a shorter distance, to go along with being easier to walk up when the mud and the white stuff appears.

It was just beginning to become dawn when Mum put me out. The sky had that dark blue edge with a pink/orange tinge to it before the sun pops up to start her day. As per usual, I was the first one out, so I cantered to the other side of my field to see who was up yet. The mist was still suspended in the valley and everything was silhouetted in black – a true autumn morning.

"Hi Tuxedo, it's nice to see you back in your winter field," said Patsy, as she hopped towards me with her little white tail bobbing up and down.

"Morning, Patsy," I replied. "Yes, I like being back here too, as I can stand under my tree when it rains so I get a little shelter, and also even though the fields are a little smaller they seem cosier. I know they're smaller because when I canter up and down I can only do about 12 strides before I'm at the end, whereas in my summer field I can do at least twice that."

"That would be 24 strides then," said Patsy, who was beginning to learn multiplications at school.

"Well done, that's correct. Where are Tom and Gina, are they still sleeping?" I asked.

"Yes," replied Patsy. "They haven't got used to the darker mornings yet."

"Oh yes we have," said Tom, who was rubbing his eyes with his paws and trying to hop at the same time. Gina, however, was more honest, taking her time, one hop and two yawns. She couldn't manage to do two things at the same time, especially at this time of the day.

"Well, what's the plan for this morning?" asked Tom.

"I'm going to walk around my field first to check it's all OK, with no surprise holes that you three may have made!" I said.

Tom, Gina and Patsy looked at each other sheepishly. "There may be a couple in the far corner," they said. With that, six paws pointed to that part of my field.

"Thank you," I said. "I knew there'd be some somewhere, but at least they aren't in the middle of my field like last year, where I could have broken my leg."

"We did listen to you," said Gina, "and we don't want you to hurt yourself. But we do get a little carried away with our digging."

As I walked around surveying my field, checking everything was in order, I heard a loud chirping sound I recognised.

I walked over to my one of my favourite trees and there was Russell the Robin, calling me over to say good morning.

"Morning, Tuxedo," he said. "How are you? Did you have a lovely summer? Wasn't the weather amazing?"

"I know," I replied. "The best summer we've had for quite a few years, I think. How was yours?"

"Good," replied Russell. "Just relaxed before getting ready for the forthcoming winter months. I think we could have quite a hard one this year, as I've noticed the leaves are beginning to change their colours already, so the first frost is not far away."

"I've noticed that too," I said. "When we were out riding the other afternoon some of the trees are now a blaze of bright red, burnt oranges and vibrant yellows. I've also noticed—" But before I could finish, a thundering of hoofs interrupted me, announcing the arrival of Mercy.

"Morning all, isn't it great to be back up here?" he said, mane flowing, tail high, making it apparent he wanted to play. "Come on, Tuxedo," he said. "Let's go burn off some energy after being in our stables all night."

I didn't need to be asked twice to play, so off we went, cantering around our fields.

Russell, Tom, Gina and Patsy all started laughing as they looked at the two of us playing tag in the early morning sun.

"Now, girls," said Tom, "you understand why we don't dig holes in the middle of the horses' fields."

After Mercy and I had had our mad half-hour, we settled down to enjoy the new grass in our fields.

As we were grazing away, I sensed something was looking at me. So I turned around and there was a sheep that I hadn't seen before; it looked a bit like Betsy but a little different, with large curly horns.

So I pottered over to introduce myself and asked who it was.

"I'm a ram," it said with an odd accent. "I've been brought here to improve the bloodline for next year's lambs."

"Where are you from?" I asked.

"My ancestors are Italian, hence my accent. My name is Romeo."

"Romeo, pleased to meet you. I'm Tuxedo," I introduced myself. "How are you settling in?"

"Some of the other animals are not that friendly, but I think it's because they don't understand me," he explained.

"I've had that problem before when I've moved from country to country. It takes a while for your accent to lose its strength. But I understand you, so stick with me and I'll make sure that the other animals start talking to you." With that, we rubbed noses, concreting our friendship.

Early that afternoon Mum came to get me for our afternoon ride. It started out like any other ride.

Mum groomed me. She had to use the harder brushes this time to get rid of some of the mud that had spattered onto my tummy after playing with Mercy earlier.

After I was all tacked up, Mum put on her hat and off we pottered.

Now, it's important to know at this point that it had been raining quite heavily for the past few days. Therefore, I knew I would have to tread carefully, as it can get quite slippery.

So off we set. It was a lovely afternoon; everything smelt fresh after the rain. We went a different way around the estate, making it more interesting as we could explore and see different things.

The sheep and the lambs had been moved to the lower pastures where the better grass was. Jeremy saw us and trotted over to see how I was. He looked more magnificent than the last time I saw him, as now his antlers were very tall. He said he was enjoying being in charge of the herd. He also seemed to have quite a few female admirers following him.

"Be careful, Tuxedo," he said. "It's slippery underfoot in places, especially on the hills, because of the rain."

"I know," I replied. "Mum's keeping me on a slightly tighter rein than normal to help me with my balance and speed, so I don't walk too fast and skid. Thank you for your concern."

"That's OK, but listen to your mum," said Jeremy. "Don't be too cocky today. You know what you can be like."

"Understood," I replied. "See you soon, love to Charlotte and Jessica."

As Mum and I walked, I must admit I did want to go for a canter, but I took on board what Jeremy had said, so I slowed down and concentrated on where I was putting my hoofs.

Things were going well until we came down a slope we hadn't been down for a while and then everything happened so fast. My legs suddenly decided to go in all four different directions; the front ones slid straight out in front of me, my back legs went straight behind me. It felt like I was doing the horse splits. The next thing I know I'm face down in the mud. Yes, I did a face plant.

Mum had to get off me, as I wouldn't have been able to stand back up if she was still on my back.

Then things went pear-shaped. Mum went to stand up; she slipped on the muddy slope and slid back into me, making me fall into the mud again. We both laughed now covered in mud.

Mum stood up and so did I, both being very careful where we were treading and not rushing it. She then went to walk up the slope and slid back into me again. I thought to myself, This could be a very long afternoon.

I stayed where I was. I wasn't going to move anywhere until I knew Mum wasn't going to slip again. With that, she took an alternative route, where there was more grass than mud, so she could get her footing. Once she had stopped sliding around, she beckoned me to follow in her footsteps, which I did very carefully.

At last, we made it to the top of the slope and began to walk back to the stables, Mum leading me slowly by my reins. She didn't get back on me for safety reasons as I could have slipped again and she was covered in mud, which would have dirtied my saddle.

So with mud dripping from us both we arrived back at the stables. At first, everybody was concerned that we may have hurt ourselves, but Mum reassured everyone we hadn't. She retold the story and everyone started to laugh, as we looked very funny. I had mud everywhere including in my ears, my eyelashes and nostrils.

Once Mum had removed my tack, she gave me a wash down with warm water, and then put my thick rug on so I would not get cold.

Back in my stable all snuggled up and about to have my dinner, thinking it had again been a surprising day full of adventures and meeting new friends, I decided to definitely stay away from the muddy slope for a while.

Before I started my dinner, I checked to see that Romeo was OK. He was — he had settled down on some hay bales next to my stable, happily munching away. I think over the next few months we will become the best of friends… we will become inseparable. With that, Russell flew in to share my dinner.

Little Pearl of Wisdom for October

Enjoy autumn with its mists and fogs, and the fantastic ever-changing colours of the leaves.

Sometimes things can go wrong, but learn from them so you don't make the same mistake twice.

Listen to others when they give good advice.

November

Losing friends, having fun

dealing with anger and coping with sadness

Firstly, let me say it has had to have been the worst morning ever. It started with going up to my field with Mum, the rain pouring down, making me walk sideways with my head down as it was hitting me quite hard. All the other horses looking out from their snuggly stables thinking to themselves. Glad it's Tuxedo and not us going out just yet.

I don't mind going out in this. I had my waterproof rug on and it gave me a chance to catch up with Oscar.

At the moment, the only problem was the amount of mud in my field. As it had been raining heavily for a few days, the mud was now in parts past my knees.

Even Mum kept on getting stuck in the mud with her boots, nearly falling over a few times.

As she opened my gate with the rain lashing down, I took shorter strides, careful not to slip on the little slope down into my field. For a few seconds, all you could hear was the squelching of my hoofs and of Mum's boots as we walked in the thick mud.

Mum cuddled me to say goodbye and before she went to work said in an authoritative voice, "Now, no running around with Mercy today. The mud is very thick in both your fields and I don't want you losing another shoe, Tuxedo."

I snorted and turned, walking slowly as I had to pick my hind legs up out of the cold mud. I had to lift them higher than usual so I wouldn't get stuck.

I made a note to self to be careful as I walked today, as I knew if I lost a shoe, Mum wouldn't be very impressed with me.

It took ages for the sun to come up today. I even think she had decided to have a lie in. The sky was dark and dull and, what was really odd, there was no wind. At this time of the year there is always a wind.

Another thing I noticed: none of the other horses had come out into their fields. Not even Mercy.

I shivered, not from the cold but from a feeling that something didn't seem right; even the grass didn't taste as nice today. I stood facing the stables, waiting for Mercy to come up and join me.

It seemed ages before anyone came up, even though it was busy with lots of cars and lorries going backwards and forwards along the driveway to the stables.

"Oh Tuxedo, oh Tuxedo!" I turned around to see Patsy hopping towards me in floods of tears.

I bent my head down so I was on the same level as her. "Patsy, come here, poppet, what's the matter? What's made you so upset?"

"Oh Tuxedo, I know it happens to us all in the end, but Mo has passed on, she's gone to horse heaven."

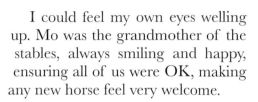

I could feel my own eyes welling up. Mo was the grandmother of the stables, always smiling and happy, ensuring all of us were OK, making any new horse feel very welcome.

"Oh, that's very sad news," I said, "but we know she had been quite sick for a while and I think just recently she'd been in a little pain."

"I know," replied Patsy, finding it hard not to cry. "She was just so lovely, I'm going to miss her so much."

"I'm going to miss her too," I said, "but it's important to remember her as the special horse that she was and we have all those lovely memories of us all together; they will always be with us. She's now in a place where there is no pain, and she can canter and play with all the other horses there."

As Patsy was crying, I bent down a little further so I could give her a little kiss on the cheek to reassure her. "Patsy, it's OK to cry and be sad; it's our feelings telling and showing us how much we cared about her. So cry, darling Patsy." So she did, while I stayed and comforted her.

After Patsy's sobs had become hiccups and her breathing came back to normal, she said, "Thanks, Tuxedo, for explaining everything. I don't feel so sad now."

With that, a light breeze rustled through the trees. Both Patsy and

I knew it was Mo saying goodbye. "Bye, Mo," we both said. "Have a safe journey, we love you."

With that, a tear sprang into my eye, but I knew it was a happy tear; it was a fairy kiss from Mo.

Patsy and I stood there for a while remembering what a kind and special horse she was. After a while, we heard the clip clop of all the other horses making their way up to their fields, walking slowly with their heads hung low, each remembering Mo in their own way.

Mercy made his way through his field, having to pick his legs up quite high as well, as he had a lot more mud in his field than mine.

I made sure Patsy was OK before going over to see Mercy.

As Mercy and I walked to meet each other halfway, all you could hear was lots of squelching noises as our hoofs went in and out of the thick mud.

"Morning, Tuxedo," said Mercy. "I suppose you've heard about poor old Mo?"

"Yes, Patsy told me," I said. "But we know she's in a pain-free place now and she wouldn't want us to be sad. She always said, 'Make sure that you live life to the full and enjoy it.' So I think we need

to have a day of games, as that is what she would have done." As you can see, I had totally forgotten about what Mum had said to me at the beginning of the morning!

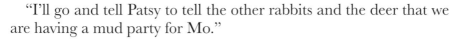

"Brilliant idea," said Mercy. "I'll go and spread the word to the other horses."

"I'll go and tell Patsy to tell the other rabbits and the deer that we are having a mud party for Mo."

With that decided, we all started running around our fields, making the mud even muddier. The rabbits and the deer joined in, and then the party really got started. Everyone rolling around in the mud, kicking it to each other, to see who could get the muddiest. It was so much fun.

As the afternoon wore on and began to get cooler, the deer and the rabbits bid farewell, but they all thanked us and agreed it had been a great party to remember Mo.

As the mums started to walk up to collect their horses and bring them in for the evening, they couldn't understand why we were all so muddy; they presumed that something must have spooked us during the day.

However, I knew I had some explaining to do to Mum, as I saw her walking towards me. "Tuxedo, what on earth have you done? You are covered in mud; it's in your eyes, nostrils, ears and even on your eyelashes. I've never seen you look such a mess. And your field looks like it's been ploughed by a tractor. I think an explanation is in order."

I tried to look bashful at this point, as she tried to put my head collar on, but she gave up as I had too much mud on my face; it just wasn't going to do up. With my head held low, knowing I was in trouble, we started to walk back to the stables.

That's when she noticed. "Tuxedo, what did I tell you this morning? Not to lose a shoe, and what have you done? Lost a shoe. I bet that's because you've been yahooing no doubt around your field with Mercy." She then tutted, so I knew I was in trouble.

I nudged her and kissed her hands to tell her I was sorry, and we continued on our way.

The mud by this stage had dried and was beginning to really itch. I couldn't wait to get my wet and muddy rug off. Today had been a rollercoaster day full of emotions.

As Mum groomed me, getting rid of all the mud that had stuck to me, it gave me a chance to reflect on all the things I had felt today. Sadness about Mo, joy and happiness playing with everyone in the mud, and also a little angry with myself for being careless and losing a shoe, especially in that kind of mud, which I know sticks like glue and pulls them off.

I felt much cleaner after being groomed. Mum fetched me a clean rug to keep me warm, giving me my goodnight cuddle and dinner. I cuddled her back, saying I was so lucky to have her as my mum and I was sorry for losing my shoe.

As I snuggled down I realised I was very tired, as it had been a big day emotionally as well as physically. It didn't take very long for my eyelids to close and then I was in a deep sleep dreaming of playing with Mo.

Little Pearl of Wisdom for November

Feelings and emotions are part of life. It's OK to be sad and angry as long as you control them, respect them and move on. If you lose someone special, remember the person with fond memories.

If you get angry with yourself, learn from your mistakes. It's your fault, nobody else's, so move on and try not to make the same mistake again.

If you are feeling a little down, play with your friends; they will always cheer you up, mine always do, and try not to get your wellington boots stuck in the mud.

the stable christmas party
and meeting the man in the red suit

A ll you could see first thing this morning was the warm air coming out of the horses' nostrils as they breathed.

"Look, I'm a dragon," said Mercy, snorting noisily.

"You do look quite scary, actually," I said.

It was jolly cold this morning. Mum had had to break the ice off my water bucket so I could have a drink, as it had frozen over overnight and the ground was now solid with the holes of mud being iced over.

"I'm glad I've got my extra-thick, spotty rug back on," I said. "That wind is bitter."

"I'm glad I've got my winter rug on too," replied Mercy, still trying to be a dragon.

"Morning, boys," said Tom, as he hopped over trying to miss the ice holes. "It's a bit chilly, isn't it? What have you been up to?"

After the mud party and losing my shoe, I'd decided not to play around too much, as I didn't want to trip or fall down any of the holes and hurt my leg or lose another shoe.

"Not much," I said. "I've been lying low, pottering around and just been nibbling on the grass; it's not as tasty as before, but it's OK." Haven't seen you for ages; where are Patsy and Gina?"

"Oh, they're getting ready for the party tonight," said Tom.

"Party, what party?" I asked.

"It's the annual stable party; everyone's invited," said Jeremy, who had just turned up looking even grander than before.

"That sounds like fun," I said. "I'm looking forward to it."

The rest of the day was pretty uneventful, but you could feel the excitement in the air, as something exciting was going to happen later.

It was starting to get a lot cooler, with an icy wind beginning to blow between the horses' legs and tails. We all hate it when it's like this. So, I was relieved to see Mum earlier than usual making her way up to come and get me. I let out a noisy neigh, as I was looking forward to getting back into the warmth of my stable.

As usual, once we got into the stable, Mum groomed me and got rid of the mud on my coat. The mud seemed to be getting worse. Maybe as there was now more mud than grass in my field.

So now, with my clean, thick pyjama rug on, Mum went to get my dinner. She put extra carrots in it tonight, so I gave her extra carrot kisses to say thank you. After our goodnight cuddles, Mum left and I started to eat my extra-special dinner.

As I was munching, I noticed that the wind had stopped and I wondered when the party was going to get started.

As you know, my stable looks out across the yard, so I popped my head over the door to see if anything was happening yet.

As I was looking out, I noticed a bright white light in the sky that seemed to be getting closer and closer, and brighter and brighter. As I stared, looking at it, my eyes at the same time seemed to be getting larger and larger; I'd never seen anything like it before. As it got nearer, I saw a bright red light at the front, guiding this big object through the sky.

I then noticed Romeo, Tom, Patsy, Gina, Jeremy, Jessica, Charlotte, Howard, Oscar, Betsy, Lola and Lily, as well as all the other animals on the estate, were making their way laughing and joking as they went into the yard.

Then all the horses started neighing. "He's on his way, he's nearly here, he's on his way." I could feel the excitement mounting around me.

"Who's arriving? Who's arriving?" I asked, as now the bright red light was only a few metres away.

"It's Father Christmas, it's Father Christmas," said Mercy, getting very excited and running around his stable.

I couldn't believe what I saw next. The red nose belonged to a deer that looked very much like Jeremy and he had eight other deer friends with him, but they didn't have his bright red nose. They were pulling what looked like Mum's car but without the wheels on it. Later on I found out it was called a sleigh.

In the driver's seat was a large man in a red suit, with a very long white beard and moustache. He had a loud laugh and friendly, twinkling eyes.

In a loud voice, he turned around to his team of little people, the elves, who are his helpers, and instructed them to open all the horses' stable doors so the party could begin.

So with all the doors open, we all stepped out. I couldn't believe what was happening; everybody was laughing and dancing with each other. Mercy said, "Come on, Tuxedo, let's get some horse grooves happening."

"I'm not a very good dancer," I said.

"I bet you are," said Patsy. "You've got Latin blood in you being from Argentina, you should be an amazing mover and groover."

"I must admit I do like a bit of a boogie," I said; then I began to dance, shaking my booty and tail. With that, all the other animals joined in. "I'm just having the best time," I said to Patsy.

"Tuxedo," said Jeremy, "let me introduce you to Father Christmas

and my cousin Rudolph. He's the one with the bright red nose at the front, in charge of the sleigh."

"Father Christmas, what an honour to meet you. I've heard so much about you. I can't believe you are here with us. And Rudolph, you have such an important job guiding Father Christmas around the world on this very special night."

"I know, it's a big responsibility," explained Rudolph, "and my red nose comes in very handy, as it helps us to see where we are going. I also have a great team of reindeer and the elves are the best navigators."

"Tuxedo, I've heard you've been a very good horse this year," said Father Christmas.

"Well, I've tried to be," I said.

"I've heard that you always make sure all the other animals, big or small, are OK and are made to feel welcome and you ensure that they have everything they need. If not, then you have offered your food and shelter to them, along with sharing your experiences and new-gained knowledge along the way. You are a very special horse, Tuxedo. You bring a lot of joy and love into the lives of everyone that you meet. That is a very special gift to have. It is an honour for me to meet you."

"Mercy, Romeo, look, I've just had my photo taken with Father Christmas!" I said, showing my two best friends my picture.

As everyone was laughing and joking, I noticed that the snow was beginning to fall again.

"It's snowing, it's snowing!" I said. "How exciting!" But then a worried thought came over me. "Won't our mums know we've been out of our stables, as our hoof prints will be in the snow and give us away?"

"No," said Father Christmas. "It's going to snow very heavily tonight, so by the time your mums come down in the morning, all will be back to being pristine, no evidence at all of our party tonight. It will always be our secret. So, with that said, it's time for everyone to go back into their own stables. My elves will come round to make sure you are all safe and secure back in your homes."

Once we were all back in, Father Christmas waved a cheery goodbye. Rudolph lit up his nose and they were off to bring joy and happiness to another festivity.

It didn't take me long to fall asleep as the snow was now falling heavily, as Father Christmas had predicted, and everything fell into a silence.

When I woke up the following morning, there was so much snow. And everyone had brightly coloured parcels outside their stable doors. Wow, what a treat!

Mum couldn't get her car down the drive this morning due to the amount of snow, so she walked along the lane, all wrapped up in thick scarves and a woolly hat. All I could see were her eyes.

When she reached my stable she said, "Happy Christmas, Tuxedo, and look you've got presents left from Father Christmas; you must have been a very good boy this year,

which you have, and you're always my gorgeous boy."

Once inside my stable she opened up my presents. I got a new thick winter rug, with bright red tartan squares on it, some shampoos and conditioners for my mane and tail, some apple-flavoured treats and a big bag of carrots.

Wow, what an amazing year it's been. I've met so many new friends and discovered things about the countryside I didn't know. I wonder what next year holds. With that, Mum gave me some of my new treats, cuddled my neck and whispered in my ear, "Tuxedo, are you ready for your next adventure? We're going to where the purple heather comes from."

Little Pearl of Wisdom for December

The best present you can give is friendship

Enjoy life, surround yourself with people you love, laugh, be true to yourself, and be generous to others.

Learn about many different things and share your experiences with your family and friends.

Play in the outdoors, enjoy and savour the different seasons, wrapping up warm in winter, and wearing shorts and t-shirts in the summer.

Remember I love you. Tuxedo rules.

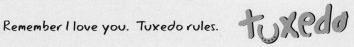

From
Tuxedo's desk

This is where I get to sincerely thank Steve and Katie, for all their help, patience and guidance in producing my book; without them, it could not have been accomplished.

Not only have they been my best friends but also as a team we have achieved far more than I could ever have wished for.

So remember with great friends and teammates you can fulfil your ambitions and reach your goals.

Thank you both.

tuxedo

W : tuxedostales.co.uk

Steve Oakes *Designer*

Steve has been working with Tuxedo on bringing his book to life and is responsible for the design and layout of this book as well as all the promotional material.

Steve is a graphic designer based in West Sussex and owner of Turquoise Creative, which is a creative design agency. Steve has over twenty years' experience in the graphic design, publishing and advertising industry working for the likes of Marks & Spencer, Royal Opera House, Rentokil Initial, Thorntons Chocolates and Yahoo.

Steve has a huge passion for creativity and is a family man who loves sport, photography, travelling and spending time outdoors… and all things turquoise.

To see examples of Steve's work please visit:
www.turquoise-creative.co.uk

E : steve@turquoise-creative.co.uk

Katie Tunn *Illustrator*

Katie Tunn is a contemporary artist based in the far north of the Isle of Skye in Scotland.

Trained at Central Saint Martins in London, she specialises in portraits of both humans and horses and her subjects range from MPs to polo ponies. Previous clients have included the British Army and the Royal Estate.

Katie regularly contributes pictures to the annual Audi Polo Awards and her drawings are owned by top polo professionals such as Adolfo Cambiaso and Facundo Pieres. She is also the namesake and trophy donor of the Katie Tunn Farewell Trophy at the Royal Berkshire Polo Club.

Aside from art, Katie has a keen interest in wildlife and nature, inspirations that are found in abundance on Skye. This is Katie's first commission as a children's book illustrator and she has enjoyed the chance to bring Tuxedo and his countryside friends to life on these pages. Should you wish to discuss an artwork idea or place a commission please contact Katie.

E : katie_tunn@hotmail.com

tuxedo's tales

Little pearls of wisdom from a horse's point of view

I hope you enjoyed reading my stories and meeting all my friends.

Have a look at my photo album on the next page.

My photo album

Having my afternoon snooze

Catching up with Mercy over a munch of hay.
His racing name is No Mercy.
He has 3 wins, 6 seconds and 5 thirds.
But now enjoying his retirement like me.

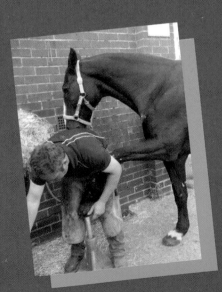

Uncle Rick replacing my shoes